Transportation & Communication Series

Ships and Boats

Arlene Bourgeois Molzahn

Enslow Publishers, Inc.

40 Industrial Road   PO Box 38
Box 398   Aldershot
Berkeley Heights, NJ 07922   Hants GU12 6BP
USA   UK

http://www.enslow.com

To my grandson, Nick, whose thoughtfulness, intelligence, and enthusiasm never cease to amaze me.

Copyright © 2003 by Enslow Publishers, Inc.

All rights reserved.

No part of this book may be reproduced by any means without the written permission of the publisher.

Library of Congress Cataloging-in-Publication Data

Molzahn, Arlene Bourgeois.
    Ships and boats / Arlene Bourgeois Molzahn.
       p. cm. — (Transportation & communication series)
    Summary: Discusses the different types of ships and boats, from canoes to warships.
    Includes bibliographical references and index.
    ISBN 0-7660-2025-8
    1. Ships—Juvenile literature. 2. Boats and boating—Juvenile literature. [1. Ships. 2. Boats and boating.] I. Title. II. Series.
    VM150 .M65 2003
    623.8'2—dc21
                            2002008920

Printed in the United States of America

10 9 8 7 6 5 4 3 2 1

To Our Readers: We have done our best to make sure all Internet Addresses in this book were active and appropriate when we went to press. However, the author and the publisher have no control over and assume no liability for the material available on those Internet sites or on other Web sites they may link to. Any comments or suggestions can be sent by e-mail to comments@enslow.com or to the address on the back cover.

Every effort has been made to locate all copyright holders of material used in this book. If any errors or omissions have occurred, corrections will be made in future editions of this book.

Illustration Credits: *The Complete Encyclopedia of Illustration* by J.G. Heck, p. 21; Corel Corporation, pp. 10, 14, 15, 16 (top), 18, 22 (top), 23, 24, 28, 30, 32, 33, 34 (top), 35 (bottom), 36, 38 (bottom), 39, 40, 42, 43; Dover Publications, Inc., pp. 4, 6, 7 (bottom), 8 (bottom), 9, 27; Judith Edwards, p. 20 (top); Enslow Publishers, Inc. diagram using Corel image, p. 12; Hemera Technologies, Inc. 1997-2000, pp. 1, 2, 5, 7 (top), 8 (top), 11, 13, 16 (bottom), 17, 19, 20 (bottom), 22 (bottom), 25, 29, 31, 34 (bottom), 35 (top), 37, 38 (top), 41; Courtesy of the United States Naval Institute, p. 26.

Cover Illustration: Corel Corporation

Contents

The *Titanic*

On the morning of April 10, 1912, the ship *Titanic* left on its first voyage. It was sailing from England to New York City in the United States. The *Titanic* was the largest ship that had *ever* been built.

People called the *Titanic* "The Wonder Ship" because it seemed to have everything on it. There were places to eat, a gym, and a swimming pool. It had many fancy rooms for passengers on the upper decks. It also had rooms down in the lower part of the ship. There were about 2,200 people on the *Titanic* for its first trip.

People thought the *Titanic* was the safest

In the early 1900s, the *Titanic* (left) was the largest ship ever built. It was nearly 882 feet long, and it was as tall as an eleven-story building.

Here people are walking on the deck of the *Titanic*.

Some of the bedrooms on board the *Titanic* looked like this.

ship ever built. They believed the ship could not sink because it had two bottoms. One bottom was built inside the other. The lower part of the ship was divided into sixteen different rooms, or compartments. Each compartment was supposed to be watertight. If one compartment started to flood, its steel door was closed. Then the water stayed in that compartment and would not flood the rest of the ship. The ship would not sink even if four of its compartments filled with water.

On April 14, 1912, four days after it left England, the *Titanic* had reached the waters off the coast of Canada. These waters were cold and icy. Icebergs, huge mountains of ice that break off of glaciers, were floating in the water.

It was 11:40 P.M. when the lookout on the *Titanic* spotted what seemed like a mountain of ice straight ahead.

He shouted, "Iceberg ahead!"

The crew member below tried to turn the ship, but it was too late. The iceberg ripped open the side of the great ship.

Many people on the *Titanic* were asleep. Others were in the ship's ballroom.

The captain of the ship checked out the damage. Water was flooding six compartments. The captain knew the ship would sink. He gave

The *Titanic* sank into the ocean.

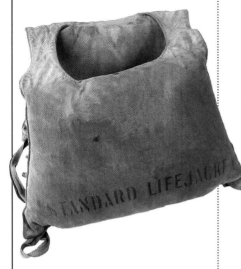

orders to radio for help. He ordered the crew to wake everyone.

The captain ordered the passengers into the lifeboats, but many did not listen to him. They did not believe that the *Titanic* would sink.

There were only enough lifeboats on the ship for 1,100 people. Many of these boats were only half full when the crew lowered them into the water. Many people who were in the bottom of the ship did not reach the top deck.

Many people ran for the lifeboats and were rescued.

The *Carpathia* came to the rescue.

Ships in the area did not reach the *Titanic* in time to save many of the passengers. The great ship slipped into the ocean at 2:20 A.M. There were 1,517 passengers and crew still aboard or drowning in the icy water. At 4:00 A.M., the ship *Carpathia* arrived to pick up the passengers in the lifeboats. Only 707 people, mostly women and children, were saved.

In 1985, scientists found the wreckage of the *Titanic*. The ship lay in two pieces on the ocean floor.

Chapter 2

Ships and Boats of Today

Parts of a Ship

Ships are like small cities that can move from place to place across the water. Ships have to be strong enough to handle winds and waves. A modern ship of today has four main parts: the hull, the engines, the propellers, and the rudder.

The hull is the outside shell of the ship. Some ships have two hulls, one built inside the other. The bottom of a ship is divided into several compartments. If an accident happens, huge watertight doors close off the damaged compartment. This stops the water from flooding the rest of the ship.

Ships (left) today come in all shapes and sizes.

The diagram below shows some parts of a ship. Masts are long poles that hold sails. The funnel is the ship's smokestack. The captain and the crew steer the ship from the bridge. Derricks are lifting devices that lower and lift cargo from the holds. The engine room is where the engine is kept in good condition. Cargo is stored below the deck in the holds.

The front of the ship's hull, called the bow, is usually pointed to help the ship travel quickly through the water. The back of the hull, called the stern, is usually rounded which makes the water flow smoothly behind the ship.

Most ships have one of the following engines: steam turbines, gas turbines, or diesel engines. The biggest ships have steam turbines. Steam from the boilers makes the wheels of the

turbine spin. The turbine makes the propellers move.

A ship has a propeller that moves it through the water. Propellers are sometimes called screws. As the propeller turns, it screws itself through the water. This pushes the ship forward. Small ships usually have one propeller. Very big ships can have as many as four propellers.

The rudder is a large flat piece of metal. It is under the water at the back of the ship. It can move from side to side. The rudder is connected to the helm, or steering wheel, of the ship. By moving the rudder, the ship can be turned to go in any direction.

Propellers help make ships and boats move forward.

Kinds of Ships

Ships that carry goods, or cargo, from port to port are called freighters, cargo ships, or merchant ships. These ships carry goods such as wheat, corn, coffee, paper products, and many other goods.

Ships that carry oil are called tankers.

Freighters are big ships that carry goods.

Tankers carry oil across the oceans.

Modern tankers are built with two hulls. This protects the ocean in case the outer tanker hull is damaged.

Barges have box-shaped hulls and no engines. They are used to move all types of cargo. They are pulled or pushed by tugboats.

Tugboats are powerful boats that help move larger ships. Tugboats can tow big cruise ships. They also help ships in and out of their docks.

Ferries are used to carry people across the water. They can also carry cars, trucks, and trains. Ferries come in all sizes. Sometimes they take the place of bridges and tunnels to connect roadways and cities.

Cruise ships are passenger ships. People can cross the oceans on them and go to many different places. Passengers on a cruise ship can do many things. They can see movies, use fitness centers, go dancing, swim in a pool, and use their computers. Large meals are served eight times a day on most cruise ships.

Another type of ship is the fishing boat. Fishermen and women take boats out on lakes and on the ocean. They catch many types of fish. They also catch lobsters, oysters, and other shellfish. Workers are needed to get the fish ready for stores all over the world.

The navies of many countries have aircraft carriers, battleships, destroyers, guided missile cruisers, and submarines. All navy ships are used to protect the country and to protect other ships at sea.

Boats are smaller than ships. They are used mostly for fun on rivers and small lakes. The motorboat and the sailboat are two types that can be used.

Tugboats may look small, but they work hard.

Ferries can carry people and cars across water where there are no bridges.

This little tugboat is helping the cruise ship into port.

Cabin cruisers are motorboats with small cabins on them. People can keep out of the sun or the rain by staying in the cabin. Some cabins are big enough for people to sleep overnight in them.

Houseboats are large boats that are like houses. They travel slowly on calm rivers or lakes.

Yachts are the largest type of motorboat. They have bedrooms, a dining area, and places for people to play games. Many have radar, radiotelephones, and other electronic equipment.

Sailboats have large sails. The wind blowing on these sails moves the boat on the water. Some large sailboats have motors in them so they can travel even when the wind is not blowing.

Canoes, kayaks, and rowboats are some of the smallest boats. People take them from place to place on top of their cars or on boat trailers. These types of boats are used on small lakes and rivers.

Sailboats are powered by wind.

Many people enjoy canoeing on lakes and rivers.

Chapter 3

The First Ships and Boats

The first boat was probably a log that someone found floating. That person may have hung on to the log and floated down a river. Later, people learned to build rafts by tying logs together with strong vines.

Next came the dugout boat. The inside of a log was burned out. Then the center of the log was scraped out with a sharp stone. These boats were heavy to carry on land and not easy to steer in the water.

In North America, American Indians learned to make boats called canoes. They were made from birch bark. These were lightweight and could be easily carried over land. They were

This crew member (left) is wrapping up a sail on a mast.

Some early boats were made of logs with the center dugout. This dugout boat is on wheels to help people move the boat over land.

much easier to control in the water than a dugout boat, but they were not as strong.

In countries where there were few trees, boats were made of animal skins. The skins were sewn into bags. The bags were filled with air and tied together to make a raft.

In other countries, boats were made from plants with hollow stems called reeds. Bundles of reeds were tied together to make a raft that would float.

All these types of boats needed someone to paddle them when going upstream.

Thousands of years ago, people of Egypt discovered how to use wind power. They put sails on their boats. They also began building their boats with wooden boards, or planks. Soon larger, stronger, and safer boats were being built.

Several groups of people made these early ships better. The sails of a ship are attached to a long pole called a mast. These ships had one square sail. The Phoenicians and the Greeks were the first to build ships with two masts. Then they could use two sails on their ships. The additional sail was a small triangular sail on the rear mast, near the stern, which is the back part of the ship. It made steering easier. Later, to go faster, the Greeks and Phoenicians built ships with as many as four sails. A ship

This is a picture of an early Greek ship. People had to use long oars to make it move.

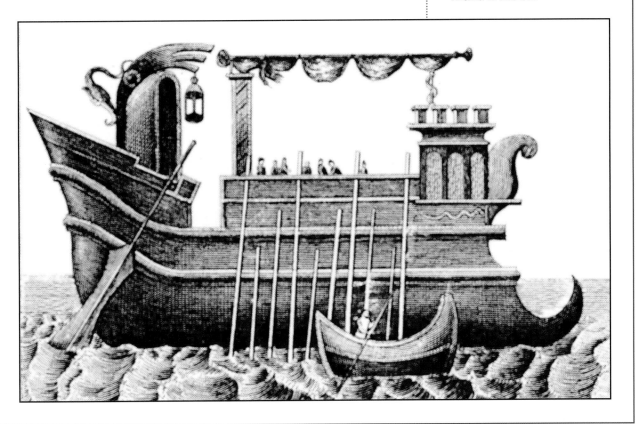

These junks have their sails down while at dock.

Vikings had boats that looked like this.

with four sails could travel faster than a ship with only two sails.

While people in Europe were experimenting with sails and masts, the Chinese were building big oceangoing ships. These ships were called junks. They had sails that could be moved to let the ship sail almost into the wind.

About 2,100 years ago, Romans built large ships for trading along the Mediterranean Sea. Their ships could carry a lot of cargo and as many as 1,000 passengers. People traveling on these ships lived on the open decks. Little tent-like shelters were set up on deck for them to sleep at night.

The Vikings who lived in northern Europe were the best shipbuilders in the years from about 700 to 1000. Viking ships were decorated with wood carvings and were very colorful. Their boats had one large sail and as many as sixty oarsmen. Oarsmen are men who use oars to row a boat.

The *Niña*, the *Pinta*, and the *Santa María* are famous ships in history. These are the ships that Christopher Columbus and his crew sailed on during their first voyage. They were trying to find a new route to the Indies. The ships sailed across the Atlantic Ocean and reached the Caribbean Sea in 1492.

The *Mayflower* is another famous ship. It brought the Pilgrims to America in 1620. The trip took sixty-six days.

This replica of the *Mayflower* shows the kind of boat that was used in 1620 to bring the Pilgrims (top) to America.

Bigger, Better, Safer

Shipbuilders kept building ships that were bigger and stronger. But these ships needed wind or men to row them. Then in 1769, James Watt, an engineer from Scotland, invented the steam engine.

Many inventors tried to use the steam engine to power ships. Many did not work. Then an American, Robert Fulton, built a ship that he called the *North River Steamboat*. It used a steam engine designed by James Watt to power the ship's paddle wheel. In 1807, the *North River Steamboat* steamed up the Hudson River from New York City to Albany. His ship traveled 150 miles. The trip took about thirty hours and

This wavepiercing catamaran (left) gives people a smooth ride in all types of weather conditions. The shape of the hull actually pierces the waves.

Robert Fulton designed the first steamboat that was used for passenger service. Later in his life, Robert Fulton designed a steam-powered warship. The ship, *Demologos*, was launched in 1812, but was never used in battle.

included an overnight stop. The *North River Steamboat* had regular passenger service on the Hudson River in New York. Fulton's ship could only be used on bays and rivers, but it was the first passenger steamboat that worked.

In 1809, John Stevens, an American engineer, built the *Phoenix*. His ship was the first steamship to travel on the ocean. The *Phoenix* went along the Atlantic coast of the United States.

In 1819, the *Savannah* became the first steamship to cross the Atlantic Ocean. It took the *Savannah* twenty-seven and a half

Demologos

days to go from New York City to Liverpool, England. It used sails part of the way.

In 1838, the British ship *Sirius* became the first passenger steamship to cross the Atlantic between the United States and Europe using only steam power. The trip took eighteen days and ten hours.

In the 1880s, steel began to replace iron and wood in shipbuilding. Steel was stronger than iron. In 1881, the British ship, *Servia*, was the first all-steel passenger ship to cross the Atlantic Ocean.

John Stevens built the first steamship to travel on the ocean.

Ships were being built better. Propellers soon replaced paddle wheels. The propeller pushed the ship forward much better than the paddle wheels.

Newer and better engines were being made. Later several steam engines were used for one ship. Then steam turbines came into use in the 1890s. A turbine is a device that uses water, steam, gas, or wind to move a rotor. The energy made by the turbine is used to run machines.

Paddle wheels help move ships along rivers and lakes.

A German engineer, Rudolf Diesel, invented a very different type of engine in 1892. Instead of steam, this new engine used heavy oil as fuel. This engine is known today as the diesel engine. The first diesel-powered ships came into use during 1910 and 1911. They were called motorships. Soon the diesel engine replaced the steam engine on many big cargo ships.

In 1954, the United States launched, or set

afloat, the first ship that used nuclear power. It was the submarine *Nautilus*. It was in use until 1979.

In 1959, the United States launched the *Savannah*, the first merchant ship that used nuclear power. Germany, Japan, and the Soviet Union also have merchant ships that use nuclear power. The United States stopped using the *Savannah* in 1971. Nuclear-powered ships cost a lot to build and run. Nearly all the large oceangoing ships still use diesel engines today.

Many smaller ships and boats use waterjets to move. Waterjets are pumps that make a high pressure stream of water to push the hull through the water. Some ships, including some of the biggest new cruise ships, are powered by gas turbine engines. These are the same engines that airplanes use.

The first ship to use nuclear power was a submarine.

Chapter 5

Working with Ships and Boats

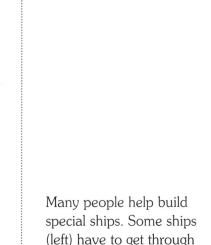

Today, much planning is needed before a ship can be built. Ship designers, called naval architects, need to know what the ship will be used for and where it will be sailing. They need to know what kind of cargo it will carry and how fast the ship will travel. The naval architect must also study government safety rules before drawing the plans for the ship.

Many people are needed to build a ship. Skilled people such as metalworkers and welders have important jobs in shipbuilding. Chemists, physicists, and engineers also have important jobs in building a large ship.

Large ships are built at shipyards. Shipyards

Many people help build special ships. Some ships (left) have to get through ice and storms.

This ship is in dry dock ready to be worked on. Dry dock is a dock where a ship is out of the water.

are factories that can be found on a waterfront. Large sections of the ship are built in factories.

These sections have the wiring and piping built into them. Giant cranes lift these sections in place. Then the sections are welded together.

The ship is launched when it is nearly finished. A steel launchway is heavily greased. The ship is then slid down the launchway into the water. Workers can now finish building the ship. Then the ship is taken on a trial run. Everything is tested to make sure that the equipment is working well. Ships usually return with a broom on their mast. This means the ship has passed all the tests. Finally, the ship is ready to be put into service.

Tugboats work hard to move big ships in and out of dock.

Many people have jobs sailing on the ships after they are built. Officers, sailors, engineers, stewards, radio operators, and medical people are needed to sail a large ship.

Many factories build boats that people use for fun. Sailboats, motorboats, canoes, kayaks, houseboats, and yachts are all made in factories in the United States. These boats provide fun for thousands of people. Building them provides jobs for many people.

The equipment used in ships and boats needs to be built. People in electrical factories are needed to make radar and radiotelephones. People in furniture factories make the furniture used in yachts and cruise ships. Stoves, refrigerators, and freezers are made for the kitchens in ships.

People are needed to operate large ocean ships. It takes a lot of training to teach anyone to operate a big ship. Tugboat

Boats are built to do many jobs. They help police (top), fishermen (middle), and firefighters (bottom) do their work.

33

These shipping crates are ready to be loaded onto a freighter.

captains must be very skilled to steer a large ship or boat into port.

Thousands of people work on the docks to load and unload cargo that large ships carry. After the cargo is unloaded, trucks or trains haul it to many places. The empty ships are then reloaded with different cargo to be taken somewhere else.

The navies of many countries provide jobs for thousands of men and women. Aircraft carriers make it possible for fighter planes to take off and land throughout the world. Battleships and destroyers are used to patrol the oceans and the coastlines of countries.

Aircraft carriers are big ships. They make it possible for planes to land and take off in the middle of an ocean.

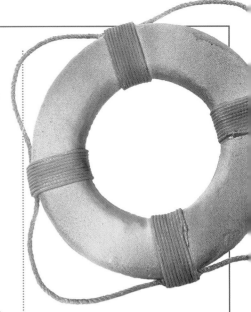

Chapter 6

Safety

Many rules have been set up to keep ships safe at sea. Ships must have watertight compartments, which are walls that can be sealed off in case of an emergency. They must have fire-fighting equipment. There must be enough lifeboats to carry all the people on the ship. There must also be enough life jackets for everyone on board. Ships passing each other must follow certain rules. Ships must keep a safe distance from other vessels.

People must use good sense when riding on boats. Never overload a small boat with people or cargo. Always wear a life jacket while on a boat. Listen to the weather forecast and watch

The white balls floating on the water (left) tell people where they can safely anchor their boats.

Lighthouses help ships by letting them know that land is near.

the skies to make sure bad weather is not coming. Do not go out in a small boat when it is foggy.

The United States Coast Guard puts floating guides called buoys in the water. Most of these buoys are either red or green. Some buoys have lights on them. These are like road signs on the water showing what route to take in and out of a harbor. Many buoys also have bells, horns, or whistles that warn boaters of danger.

Lighthouses are very useful in fog and at night.

Some buoys have a horn that sounds to warn ships during foggy weather. Lighthouses and foghorns help guide boats and ships to safety in bad weather. Coast Guard stations fly certain kinds of flags that tell boaters about weather conditions.

Chapter 7

Boat Races and Future Ships

Boat Races

There are many types of boat races. The most famous yacht race is the America's Cup. It is held every three years, and yachts from all over the world compete for a trophy. From 1851 to 1980, the United States always won the race. But in 1983, Australia won the trophy. Since then, New Zealand has won it two times. The United States has won it another three times.

There are many different boat races in the Olympic Games. The Olympics are held every four years. Men race using kayaks, canoes, and rowboats. Women race with kayaks and rowboats. It is exciting to watch as boats rowed

It takes many people (left) to win a sailing race.

People race motorboats as well.

by men and women of one's country skim swiftly over the water. It is fun to cheer as these people work hard to win an Olympic medal.

Future Ships

Shipbuilders are working to design future ships that will be faster, safer, and that will cost less to run. Ships will be built larger so that they can carry more cargo. There will be more computerized machinery on the ships. In the future, many parts of ships will be built of aluminum and other materials that do not rust.

The newest navy ships are called trimaran warships. Britain is testing this type of three-hulled ship. Ships with triple hulls have greater speed, use less fuel, and are safer in rough water. Trimaran warships can be built so they are very difficult to see on enemy radar screens. They may be the ships of the future for the United States Navy.

Men and women race with boats called sculls. These women just finished a race.

Timeline

Thousands of Years Ago—People in Egypt use sails and build boats with wooden planks; Phoenicians and Greeks build ships with two masts; Chinese build junks; Romans build large ships for trading; Vikings build better ships.

1450—Shipbuilders along the Mediterranean Sea begin using the sailing ship.

1807—Robert Fulton of the United States builds the first successful steamboat.

1819—The American ship the *Savannah* is the first steam-powered ship to cross the Atlantic Ocean.

Timeline

1836—Propellers are used to drive steamboats.

1838—The ship *Sirius* is the first to offer regular service across the Atlantic Ocean using steam power.

1897—Steam turbines are used in ships.

1910—Ships are powered by motors.

1959—The first nuclear-powered merchant ship, the *Savannah*, is built.

2010—The first trimaran ships are expected to be completed.

Words to Know

bow—The name for the front part of a ship or a boat.

cabin—A private room on a ship.

dock—To dock a ship is to bring it into a harbor so that it can be unloaded or repaired.

glacier—A large mass of ice slowly moving down a slope or over an area of land.

hull—The outside shell of a boat or a ship.

naval architect—A person who designs and draws up plans for ships and boats.

port—A place where ships and boats can load and unload; a city or town with a harbor where ships can dock.

stern—The back of a ship or boat.

upstream—At or toward the beginning of a stream or river.

vessel—Another name for a ship or boat.

watertight—Something that is watertight is said to be waterproof.

Learn More About
Ships and Boats

Books

Ditchfield, Christin. *Kayaking, Canoeing, Rowing and Yachting*. Danbury, Conn.: Children's Press, 2000.

Lincoln, Margaret. *Amazing Boats*. New York: N.Y.: Alfred A. Knopf Books for Young Readers, 1992.

Platt, Richard. *Eyewitness: Shipwreck*. New York, N.Y.: DK Publishing, 2000.

Internet Addresses

BoatSafeKids

<http://www.boatsafe.com/kids/index.htm>

This site has questions and answers about boat safety. It also has fun games.

Adventures at Sea

<http://tqjunior.thinkquest.org/6169>

Are you ready for a sea adventure? Find out on this ThinkQuest site.

Index